P9-ELT-568

COME TO THE FAIR

JANET LUNN paintings by GILLES PELLETIER

Tundra Books

Published in Canada by Tundra Books, *McClelland & Stewart Young Readers,*
481 University Avenue, Toronto, Ontario M5G 2E9

Published in the United States by Tundra Books of Northern New York,
P.O. Box 1030, Plattsburgh, New York 12901

Library of Congress Catalog Number: 97-60509

Canadian Cataloguing in Publication Data

Lunn, Janet, 1928 –
        Come to the fair

ISBN 0-88776-409-6

I. Pelletier, Gilles, 1946-   .   II. Title.

PS8573.U55C65 1997   jC813' .54   C97-930717-1
PZ7 .L86Co 1997

We acknowledge the support of the Canada Council for the Arts for our publishing program.

Design by K.T. Njo

Printed and bound in Canada

1 2 3 4 5 6   02 01 00 99 98 97

To my neighbors in Prince Edward County, Ontario, and the wonderful country fairs that happen every fall

J. L.

To my wife, Linda, whose sense of humor and insight keep me on track

G. P

It's the day of the Fair. For miles around, people are getting their prize animals, their vegetables, their cakes and preserves ready to display.

Before the sun is up, everyone in the Martin family is out and about. What a lot of bustle! Grandfather and the hired man are coaxing the pig into the wagon. Henry is keeping the horse quiet, while Martha runs with the pail of oats. George sees to the cows. Mother checks one more time to make sure the pumpkin she has been tending all summer is lodged firmly in the back of the truck. This year she is sure she will win a prize.

In Mr. and Mrs. Canarsie's field at the edge of town, the Play Fair Amusement Company is setting up. The cold, clean air carries the ringing of hammers and the shouts of workmen far out into the country. As if by magic, the bright, striped tents and the merry-go-rounds spring up in the empty field.

The trumpets blare, the drums boom. Here comes the parade to open the Fair. How Martha would love to drive a tractor in the parade the way her friend Marc does. George and Henry like the cowboys even more than the tractor. It's hard to believe the cowboys are really Father's friends, Mr. LeBlanc and Mr. Elliott.

At the fairground, the farmers are busy scrubbing and brushing their animals to a fine shine. The whole animal tent smells like a fresh, clean barn.

Martha and Henry and George and Pete, the dog, head straight for the food tent. The tables are crowded with cakes and pies, with pickles, jams, jellies, fruit and vegetables: watermelons and apples, fat squashes, glowing ears of corn, ripe tomatoes and deep purple eggplants. It's so hard to look at all the delicious food set out for the judges and not to be able to eat it.

The craft tent is beautiful. Quilts of every imaginable color and pattern cover the walls. Warm, flowered hooked rugs are displayed on the tables and on the ground.

Noontime and the sun is hot when the sulky races are on. People crowd into the grandstand and along the fence to watch the high steppers, and root for their favorite drivers.

The sulky horses are resting in their corral. The people are watching from the hillside as the dairy cows, all groomed and polished, are paraded past the judges. The Martin children are sure that George's favorite heifer will win a ribbon.

At last it's time to judge the giant pumpkins. Mother has been waiting anxiously all day. Such pumpkins! So enormous! So heavy! As Mother's gets weighed, the whole Martin family cheers, even Pete.

Evening has come. Everyone gathers at the bandstand to hear The Country Vagabonds play all the old favorite songs on their guitars and accordions and fiddles. People sing; they dance; they clap to the music. What a happy time it is! Even Pete is content.

The Fair ends, as it does every year, with a glorious display of fireworks. The Martin family drives toward home, stopping just far enough along to get a good view. They talk about the Fair. Mother's pumpkin won a blue ribbon and George's heifer won a red one. It has been a wonderful day.